This book belongs to:

....

EDGAR

THE LION WHO WOULD BE A GOOD KING

by SUNNY GRIFFIN
ILLUSTRATED BY R.M. KOLDING

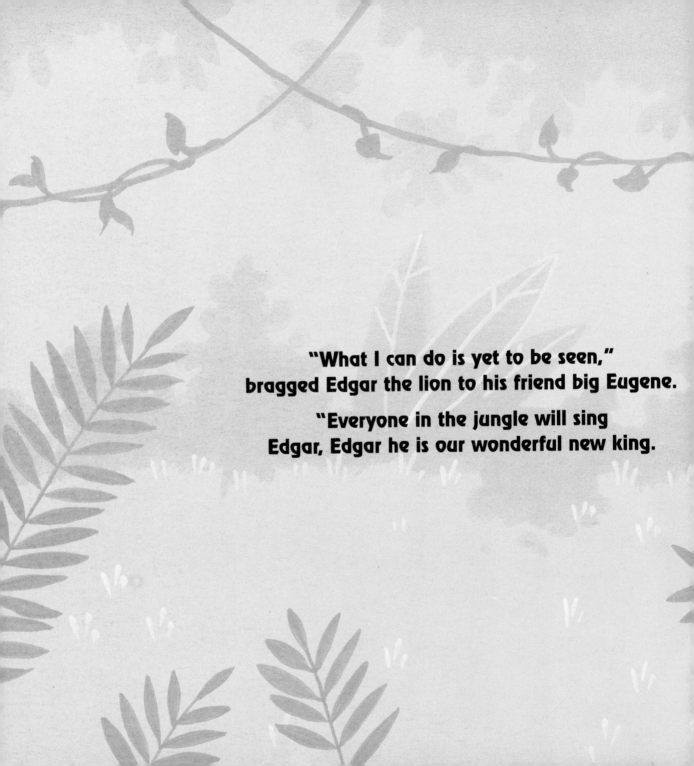

"What I can do is yet to be seen,"
bragged Edgar the lion to his friend big Eugene.

"Everyone in the jungle will sing
Edgar, Edgar he is our wonderful new king.

He said goodbye
and started
merrily out alone...
but it wasn't long
until he heard a
big growling groan.

Being a cat,
curiosity got the
better of him.
He peeked through
the thick jungle grass
but the light was
too dim.

If I get closer
he thought I can see
what's going on.
I'll just take a
quick look and
then be gone.

Suddenly he felt two
large furry paws tighten
around his chin.
Oh, no, no, no . . .
what's going to
happen to
Edgar our friend?

Edgar's eyes got big and round . . .
he was so scared he couldn't hear or speak a sound.

All around him there was
nothing but orange and yellow fur.
Everything happened so fast
it was like a blur.

In front of the real
jungle king he was thrown.
Oh no, he thought, this
is not the kind of king
I'll be when I'm grown.

The king looked quite mean and very stern
until he patted Edgar's fluffy head and
tickled his nose with a fern.

Edgar couldn't help
but laugh then he
did loudly sneeze...

the king reached down
and lifted him right
up off his knees.

"Are you the young lion who claims he is to be king?"
"Yes," said sad Edgar, "I'm really sorry
it's trouble to you I bring."

The old lion said softly . . .
"to be a king you must be old and wise.
Why a grown-up lion is twice your size.

Remember, everyone's equal in
the eyes of a good king. It's not your name
that you will want all to sing.

Now what with you, should I do" . . .
a little voice behind him spoke
and said, "your majesty the king,
I can tell you.

I'm just a little smart
monkey with no name
but I can tell you what
to do just the same.

Young Edgar is
guilty of thinking
of only his needs.
He wants to be king
it's true, but not
out of greed.

His heart is really
made of pure gold.
A wonderful king
he will make when
he grows old.

He needs someone to teach him
what is proper and right.
So in your kingdom, he will
be a welcome sight."

The old king looked into
Edgar's eager young face . . .
"it might not hurt," he said, "to have
some extra help around this place.

Stay close by my side and
learn something new each day.
Real kings don't boast or
brag but they do play."

Edgar was thrilled, having someone
to teach him was a dream come true.
Oh yes, he thought, I must thank the
monkey with no name, too.

He hugged the old king and kissed
him square on the tip of his nose . . .
but when he went to hug the monkey,
they all said, now where do
you suppose he goes?

Edgar was so anxious
to learn that he climbed right up in the king's big lap.
He wanted to be close by when the kind
old fellow awakened from his nap.